Happy Thanksgiving Hammy!

WRITTEN BY **Don Hoffman** WITH **Priscilla Palmer**

ILLUSTRATED BY **Lorraine Dey**

Written by Don Hoffman with Priscilla Palmer • Illustrations by Lorraine Dey

Art Direction by Elaine Noble

www.happythanksgivinghammy.com • www.peekaboopublishing.com

Peek-A-Boo Publishing
Part of the Peek-A-Boo Publishing Group

Printed by Shenzhen TianHong Printing Co., Ltd. in Shenzhen, China

ISBN: 978-1-943154-51-7 (Hardback)
ISBN: 978-1-943154-50-0 (Paperback)
ISBN: 978-1-943154-53-1 (eBook)
ISBN: 978-1-943154-52-4 (PDF)
ISBN: 978-1-943154-54-8 (Mobi Pocket)

10 9 8 7 6 5 4 3 2 1

HAPPY, HAPPY, HAPPY
Thanksgiving Day.

My name is Jesse and
I love Thanksgiving Day.

I am happy and thankful all day long.

I am thankful for my grandmother who knits me sweaters, even though they are scratchy.

I am happy I have a big sister
who reads to me.

I am thankful for a grandfather
who takes me fishing.

I am happy I have a dog named Lucy.

I am thankful for my dad who lets me help rake leaves. I like the bright orange ones best.

I am happy I got a good report card at school.

I am thankful for my best friend
Mika, because he doesn't mind
if I win when we race.

I am happy for the red apples
our neighbor gave us.

I'm the only one who thinks he is funny.

I am happy for the cards
the mail carrier brings.

I am thankful for my mom for baking bread.

I wish bread didn't have a crust.

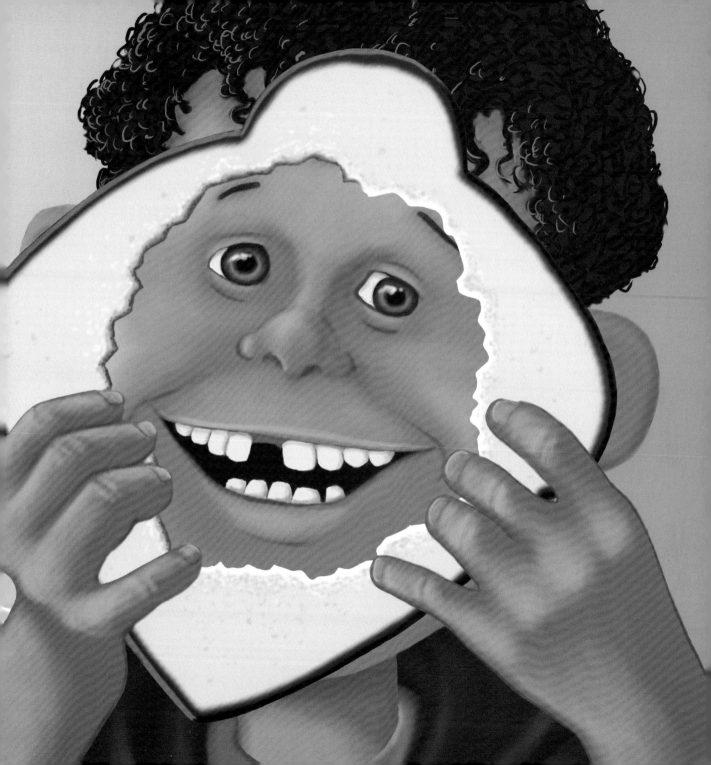

But most of all I am happy and thankful that I found my pet hamster, Hammy, who has been lost since Tuesday.

We found him in the basement under the washing machine.

He was so hungry we gave him a special Thanksgiving dinner.

Happy Thanksgiving Hammy!
Happy Thanksgiving Everyone!